The Incredible Reversing Peppermints

Dedicated to my dear friends Mike, Katherine and Claire.

A family who need no Reversing Peppermints.
I like you just the way you are.

The Incredible Reversing Peppermints

Written and illustrated
by Paul Adshead

Child's Play (International) Ltd

Swindon   Bologna   New York

Also in this series:
The secret Hedgehog
Trilby, a bird in my hat

© 1993 Paul Adshead
Published by Child's Play (International) Ltd
All rights reserved
Printed in Singapore
ISBN 0-85953-514-2

THE INCREDIBLE REVERSING PEPPERMINTS

Written and Illustrated
by
PAUL ADSHEAD

CONTENTS

CHAPTER ONE

TIME FOR A CHANGE

Patrick Marrow was feeling very sorry for himself.

Try as he might, he could not think
of one single thing to be happy about.

He sat at the
kitchen table
with his head
in his hands
and a gloomy
expression
on his face,
trying to
convince himself
that things
couldn't possibly
get any worse!

Like most boys of his age, he was always being told
just how happy he should be.

"Haven't you got wonderful parents!"
people would say. Or, "What an adorable baby
sister you've got," and things like that.

"If one more person tells me that I must be the happiest boy alive, I shall probably be sick all over them," thought Patrick to himself.

He glanced across the table at his father, whose eyes were devouring the FINANCIAL TIMES faster than his mouth could devour his breakfast, and at his mother, who was cooing with rapture at a baby in a high-chair.

"Doesn't Lizzy look a little sweetie this morning?" exclaimed Mrs Marrow, for at least the twentieth time that minute.

Patrick pretended not to hear. He thought that all babies looked the same: bald, wrinkly and rather like podgy pink slugs.

Lizzy gurgled mischievously, and the goo
that had dangled from her chin dribbled down
in a long sticky string onto her breakfast.

"The price of plastic shares has risen again,"
announced Mr Marrow from behind his newspaper.
That pleased him because he was a top business
executive with G.R.U.M.P. Co., which was short
for **G**riswald's **R**emarkably **U**seful **M**ulti-coloured
Plastics **C**ompany.

"Will you take me to the park this morning, Dad?"
asked Patrick.

"Certainly not," snapped Mr Marrow.
"I'm far too busy to waste time
with a nauseating little pimple like you!"

"Please, Dad," begged Patrick.
"After all, it is Saturday,
so you needn't go to the office."

"I've told you once," growled the voice
from behind the newspaper. "I've got an interview
for a place on the G.R.U.M.P. Co. board of
directors this Monday. I shall be working all
weekend on my plans to invent invisible smog,
so no-one will be able to see the pollution
our factories cough out while making the plastic."

He leered round his newspaper, gave his son
a smug conceited grin, and waited for him to say
how brilliantly clever he was.

Patrick said nothing. Most fathers were good fun,
and spent Saturday mornings doing exciting things
with their children, but not this father.
Not once had he said, "Let's play football!"
or "Who wants to go cycling?" or anything
like that. He was always far too busy.

"Watch my clever darling using a spoon
for the first time," said Mrs Marrow.

"Very good," grunted her husband, without even
bothering to look. "Isn't the food meant to go
in her mouth?" remarked Patrick, as he ducked
to miss a spoonful of scrambled egg that Lizzy
hurled at him. "There's more on the walls
than there was inside the eggshell!"

Mrs Marrow glared at her son,
but before she could think of a suitable reply,
Bouncer bounced in, barking loudly and wagging
his enormous tail.

Bouncer was always untidy, disobedient and clumsy.
Wherever he went, he seemed to leave a trail
of disaster in his wake.

He was the only creature Patrick knew
who could make more mess than his little sister.
But she only wet her nappies, whereas Bouncer
had an irritating habit of tiddling on people's
shoes whenever he got excited.

He was noisy too.
His bark could be quite deafening.
But, compared to the ear-splitting
screams that Lizzy could produce,
there was no competition.

In no time at all, he had slurped Lizzy's toast
off the floor and licked all the egg off the walls.
Then he leapt onto an empty chair,
stuck his large, hairy muzzle into Patrick's bowl
of cereal and guzzled the lot.

"How many times have I told you not to feed
that dog at the table?" grumbled Mrs Marrow.
"Tell him to get down this instant,
and make him stop chewing the tablecloth."

"DOWN!" shouted Patrick.

Bouncer jumped down and hid behind the door.
The trouble was, the tablecloth was still
in his mouth! Plates of buttered toast,
cups of coffee and bowls of cereal were scattered
all over the floor.

The kitchen was in complete chaos.
Lizzy suddenly filled her nappy
and started to howl and bang
her little fists
on the high-chair table,
while Bouncer ran
round and round,
trampling eggs,
cereal and marmalade
into the carpet.

At that moment, Mr Marrow folded his newspaper
and noticed what was actually going on
in the kitchen for the very first time.

"GREAT THUNDERING
BUCKETS!" he gasped,
turning to his wife,
"Can't you keep
this place tidy,
instead of sitting
on your bottom
all day doing nothing?"

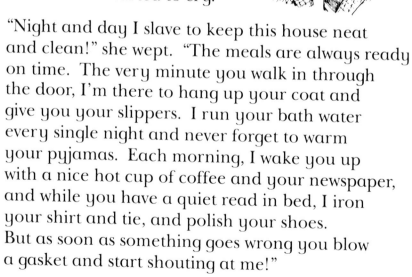

Mrs Marrow started to cry.

"Night and day I slave to keep this house neat
and clean!" she wept. "The meals are always ready
on time. The very minute you walk in through
the door, I'm there to hang up your coat and
give you your slippers. I run your bath water
every single night and never forget to warm
your pyjamas. Each morning, I wake you up
with a nice hot cup of coffee and your newspaper,
and while you have a quiet read in bed, I iron
your shirt and tie, and polish your shoes.
But as soon as something goes wrong you blow
a gasket and start shouting at me!"

"I'm off to the office," announced Mr Marrow,
brushing toast crumbs off his immaculate business
suit. "And when I get back, this room had better
be spotless, my good woman. I want my dinner on
the table, and that screeching little brat in bed."

7

"And as for you," he said, turning to Patrick,
"You'd better have that dog behaving like
a Supreme Champion, or I shall take him
to one of G.R.U.M.P. Co's factories
and have him churned into little plastic bone
shapes, for well behaved dogs to chew!"

Then he marched out of the house,
slamming the door behind him.

Patrick felt sorry for his mother.
Her hair looked straggly, her apron was stained
and crumpled, and she had a whopping big hole
in the knee of her tights!

She was really very pretty, but was always so busy
caring for her family that she never seemed to have
enough time or money left over to care for herself.

"Don't worry, Mum," Patrick said, putting his arm
around her. "I'll help you tidy the kitchen."

"Thank you, Patrick," she sniffed, wiping her eyes
on the corner of her apron. "But if you really
want to help me, you'll keep Bouncer out of my way
for a few hours. Take him for a good long walk."

Handing him a few coins from her purse,
she said, "Here, buy yourself a bar of chocolate,
it'll cheer you up!"

Patrick's mother was always kind and generous,
no matter how sad she was feeling herself,
and somehow that always made Patrick feel worse

than ever. He trudged sadly out of the door
and down the garden path. Bouncer bounded ahead,
yelping with excitement. At the gate he fastened
the leash onto Bouncer's collar and tried to make
him walk to heel. But it was hopeless. He kept
tripping up old ladies, or winding himself round
lamp posts, until Patrick felt quite dizzy.

If nothing else, Patrick was glad to get out
of the house. Even school was usually more fun
than staying at home.

"But not any longer," he sighed to himself.

Just last week, his class had been given
a new teacher called Miss Bunion, who was
very strict and didn't seem to like him much.

In a way, this wasn't very surprising. On Monday,
he had left his homework on the bus; on Tuesday,
he broke the pencil sharpener; on Wednesday, he was
late and on Thursday he lost his dinner money
through a hole in his trouser pocket.

Then, yesterday, he had been asked to define
the word 'scholastic'. Suddenly, his mind had gone
quite blank, and in a moment of panic he said
it was the type of elastic used in the girls'
regulation school knickers.

Miss Bunion had made him stand on a chair all day,
with a sign pinned to his pullover saying: "I am
a gormless little maggot!"

Patrick pushed all thoughts of school to the back
of his mind, and tried to think of something else
instead. By now he had come to the main street
of town, and, as Saturday was market day,
there was lots to see.

He wandered up and down, looking at all the little
stalls, fascinated by the amazing variety of things
for sale: boots, buttons, boomerangs, teapots,
toasting-forks, candle-snuffers, cushion covers,
white mice, ripe strawberries, trumpets,
Teddy Bears, potato peelers, night lights, kites
and knitting needles, to mention but a few.

Patrick was beginning to enjoy himself.
But Bouncer was bored stiff. He kept fidgeting
and getting into mischief. He carried off
an old man's shoe, while he was trying on
a pair of slippers. Then, he tiddled over
a lady's shopping bag.

"That does it!" said Patrick, tugging on the leash.
"We might as well go home,
before you get us into any more trouble!"

He was just turning to leave, when he saw a sign
out of the corner of his eye.
It was a perfectly ordinary sign, hanging from
one of the stalls, but for some peculiar reason,
Patrick felt compelled to read it.
It said:-

DOCTOR TAPIOCA'S INCREDIBLE REVERSING PEPPERMINTS
GUARANTEED TO REVERSE ANYBODY INTO THE OPPOSITE
OF WHATEVER THEY ARE! WILL MAKE FAT PEOPLE THIN,
SAD PEOPLE HAPPY, AND OLD PEOPLE YOUNG.

COMPLETELY SAFE AND ENTIRELY NON-TOXIC.
TO BE EATEN WHENEVER YOU FEEL
LIKE A **COMPLETE** CHANGE!"

CHAPTER TWO

DOCTOR TAPIOCA

Patrick gazed with his mouth wide open, and read the sign several times before he could really believe his eyes. It seemed too good to be true!

He couldn't think why he hadn't noticed the stall before. It looked rather like a Chinese pagoda: very tall and narrow, with lots of shelves piled high with brightly wrapped peppermints.

And the stall holder was not the kind of person you could easily forget. He was an oriental gentleman: extremely tall, with an enormous curling moustache and beard. He wore a colourful kimono with a dragon pattern on it, and a wide coolie hat.

Nervously, Patrick stepped towards the strange-looking man, wondering if he should buy one of the peppermints.
"After all," he thought to himself. "I certainly feel like a change! And anyway," he added, "Things can't get any worse. Can they?"

He reached into his pocket for the money his mother had given him, and gave a gasp of utter horror. Things HAD got worse; he had completely forgotten about the hole in his trouser pocket. All the money had gone!

"Let me introduce myself," said a loud,
booming voice.

Patrick, who was lost in the depths of despair, looked up and saw that the man in the coolie hat was leaning over and holding out his hand.

"My name is Doctor Augustine Septimus Octavian Tapioca, brilliant inventor of the Incredible Reversing Peppermints," he continued.

Patrick shook his hand politely, and said in a rather husky voice that **his** name was plain old Patrick Marrow. He looked at his watch and muttered something about having to get back home soon, so he really must be going.
"Fibber!" said the man in a kindly way, giving Patrick a friendly wink.

"I beg your pardon?" replied Patrick indignantly.

"You heard me!" laughed Doctor Tapioca. "I called you a fibber, because that's **exactly** what you are."

Patrick said nothing. It was bad enough hearing remarks like that at home, without having to put up with them from a complete stranger. He called Bouncer's name sharply and pulled on his leash.

But Bouncer was in no hurry to leave. He was gazing at the strange man with huge, adoring eyes. His tongue lolled out of his mouth in a happy grin and his tail thumped on the floor. When his master spoke he didn't even bother to turn his head.

"Not very well behaved, is he?" remarked the man.

"No, I suppose he isn't," admitted Patrick, thinking of one of Bouncer's particularly bad habits whenever he got excited.

"It's all in the mind, you see," explained the Doctor.

"I expect it'll be all over your shoes in a minute," replied Patrick, under his breath. "As I was saying," continued the Doctor. "It's all in the mind. Inside Bouncer there's a good dog just waiting to get out. What he needs is a Reversing Peppermint; guaranteed to make disobedient dogs obedient."

"I haven't any money," said Patrick.

"Oh, I know that," smiled Doctor Tapioca. "But there are far more important things than that bothering you, aren't there? I'd say you were someone who needed quite a few things reversing before you could be really happy."

"How do you know?" gasped Patrick.

"Because I'm a Doctor, of course,"
continued the man. "I examine patients like you
every single day. Say 'Ahhh'."

Patrick opened his mouth as wide as possible
and said 'Ahhhhh', while Doctor Tapioca leaned over
and peered into his left ear. Placing an enormous
thermometer under his tongue, he told him to say
'Mesembryanthemum'.

"Ooble, ooble," said Patrick.

"This is more serious than I thought!"
exclaimed the Doctor. "I shall have to prescribe
quite a few peppermints to cure you.
Eight, to be exact. That should solve
all of your problems perfectly."

"But I've already told you," groaned Patrick.
"I've lost my money."

"Oh, I expect you'll find it again before long,"
replied the Doctor, with a knowing smile.
"You can come back and pay me then."

He handed Patrick eight brightly wrapped
peppermints in a paper bag.
Each one was numbered and wrapped in a
different colour of shiny foil paper:
1-red, 2-yellow, 3-blue, 4-green, 5-orange,
6-purple, 7-pink and 8-turquoise.

"Use them carefully,"
the Doctor warned.
"Their effects
are permanent,
so be quite sure
you really want
to change someone
before you give them a peppermint."

Patrick could hardly believe it. He thanked
the Doctor and promised to return with some money
as soon as he could. Giving Bouncer an extra hard
yank on the leash, he set off for home.

"Goodbye," called Doctor Tapioca, giving Patrick
a cheery wave. Then, looking down
at the huge puddle around his feet, he shouted,
"I think that dog of yours
ought to have the first peppermint!"

Patrick did not need to be told. He had already
decided that as soon as they got to the park,
Bouncer would be given Reversing Peppermint No 1.
He could hardly wait to see the results...

CHAPTER THREE

BOUNCER

Without any doubt, the park was one of Bouncer's favourite places. So the moment he caught sight of the park gates he gave a tremendous "Woof!" and jerked so hard on the leash, that Patrick's arm was almost pulled clean off his body.

Most dogs like going to the park, because they can run around and fetch sticks for their owners to throw. But that wasn't Bouncer's idea of having fun. His idea of a good time was to give everyone else a thoroughly bad time. He would try to herd up any stray toddlers, as if they were sheep, then he would chase the whole flock of them round and round the playground until they were exhausted. If he found any toys lying around, he would either drop them in the paddling pool, or bury them in the sand pit. But his most disgusting mischief of all, was to climb to the top of the slide and tiddle down it just before someone slid to the bottom.

But this time Bouncer didn't get a chance
to misbehave. Patrick tied his leash securely
to the fence, while he opened the paper bag
containing the Incredible Reversing Peppermints.

Patrick peered into the bag, expecting them to look
as incredible as they sounded. But they didn't.
They looked perfectly ordinary. He took out
the peppermint
with the number "ONE"
printed on
its shiny red paper,
unwrapped it carefully
and sniffed it.
It even smelt
like a peppermint.
It was very disappointing. Patrick began to feel
rather glad he hadn't paid anything for them yet.

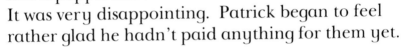

He was just wondering whether he had been the
victim of a silly joke, when he caught sight of
some writing on the outside of the peppermint bag.

WARNING
This is no ordinary peppermint! Its secret ingredients
are the result of many years of scientific research,
and it is guaranteed to reverse absolutely anybody
into their complete opposite.
Results are permanent and will not wear off.
Caution — Small children and babies can choke on hard peppermints.
To prevent accidents - peppermints can be dissolved in warm milk.

"Well, I suppose it's worth a try!" thought Patrick to himself. He tossed the peppermint to Bouncer, who leapt up excitedly, breaking his leash, caught it in mid air, and swallowed it whole.

For the next few minutes, Patrick could hardly believe his eyes. For a moment, Bouncer hung motionless in the air with a surprised look on his face. Then, all at once, brilliant red smoke poured out of his ears and he started spinning around like a gigantic hairy firework!

"Great clog-dancing cabbages!" exclaimed Patrick in amazement. "Those peppermints **are** pretty incredible after all!"

He ducked as Bouncer swooped over him
like a jet airplane. Then off he shot,
doing a double backwards loop high over the park,
leaving trails of billowing red smoke. Finally,
he buzzed a group of terrified toddlers,
landed gracefully and taxied to a halt
just in front of his master.

All this had been amazing enough, but now that
Patrick could see him properly, his mouth dropped
open and his eyes stood out on stalks.

"Bouncer, is that **really** you?" whispered Patrick
in astonishment. Bouncer gave one short, sharp
bark in answer and wagged his tail feebly.
Patrick bent down to examine him closer.

His eyes looked the same, but that was about all.
His tangled, brown hair, muddy paws and whiskers
matted with dried-on gravy had all completely
vanished. Instead, his grooming was now
as immaculate as a thoroughbred pedigree.

"It **is** you!" gasped Patrick, seeing Bouncer's
name-tag on his collar. "I wish you hadn't broken
your leash. How am I going to get you home?"

But there was no need for the leash.
Bouncer's behaviour had reversed just as much
as his appearance. He walked so close
to Patrick's heels, that whenever his master
stopped suddenly, Bouncer's nose would bump
into the back of his leg.

They walked twice right round the edge
of the playground. Once for practice, and once
because Patrick wanted to make sure everyone
had seen what an obedient dog he had.
Next, Bouncer fetched a ball for a little boy
who had lost it in some bushes, and picked a bunch
of flowers for an old lady. Finally, he scampered
around the park, picking up any litter he could
find and dropping it in the litter baskets.

Patrick could hardly wait to get back home and
see what his family thought of their incredible
wonder dog. He called to Bouncer, who came
immediately and sat by his side, looking at his master
with an alert expression.

Patrick was about to say "Home, Bouncer!",
when he had the most brilliant idea. He turned
his pocket (the one with the hole) inside-out,
and told Bouncer to smell it. Obediently, Bouncer
took several big sniffs, then waited patiently
for the next command.

"FIND!" shouted Patrick in his sternest voice.

At once, Bouncer started rushing around in circles,
sniffing at the ground. Then he hurried out
of the park gates and into the street. Here he put
his nose to the ground again and howled
in excitement. In a flash, he was off on the trail,
only glancing back to check that Patrick was still
following him. Through the streets they ran,
back towards the market, until at last Bouncer
stopped in front of a second-hand toy stall.

Patrick recognised the stall at once.
He had paused by it earlier to look at some kites.

There Bouncer stood, as still as a statue,
with his tail out straight and one paw pointing
towards a large yellow kite. Patrick knelt down
and peered behind it, and there, to his enormous
delight, he spotted the missing coins,
which had fallen out of his pocket.

Patrick scooped the money up and gave Bouncer an enormous hug. "Well done, old chap!" he said. "Just for that, I'm going to buy you the biggest bone you've ever had. But now I've found the money, I must go back to Dr Tapioca and pay for the peppermints first."

But, try as he might, Patrick could not find the mysterious Dr Tapioca or his incredible multi-coloured peppermint stall anywhere. Even when he made Bouncer sniff one of the peppermints and told him to "Find!", poor Bouncer just wandered round in circles, looking sad and confused.

It was getting quite late by now, so Patrick decided there was nothing for it but to abandon their search. After stopping off at the butcher's stall to buy Bouncer an enormous bone, they made their way back home.

As they turned into the gate, a huge black car roared down the driveway, missing both boy and dog by inches. It was Mr Marrow.

"Nearly got you that time, you dopey little worm!"

The car screeched to a halt, and he leapt out, slamming the door behind him.

"What on earth have you been doing to that awful flea-ridden mutt of yours?" he growled, glaring at Bouncer's sleek coat. "The ghastly creature looks quite clean for once."

"He is!" replied Patrick with a grin.
"And that's not all. He's as well trained
as any supreme champion, just as you ordered."

"That remains to be seen," snapped Mr Marrow.
He flung open the front door, and stormed in.

"I'M HOME!"he shouted at the top of his voice.

A loud crying noise came from upstairs
and Mrs Marrow appeared at the kitchen door,
looking tired and harrassed.

"Now you've woken Lizzy," she sighed.
"And I've only just got her off to sleep."

"Well, go and shut the little maggot up," Mr Marrow
replied. "And when you've done that, dinner had
better be ready. I'm absolutely starving!"

Mrs Marrow wiped her hands on a towel, and trudged
up the stairs.

"Fetch my slippers while you're up there!"
he shouted after her. "And you'd better be quick
about it. I've been working all day, not just
standing around peeling a few carrots like you."

As it happened, poor Mrs Marrow did not have
to fetch his slippers. Bouncer had already shot up
to Mr Marrow's room, and dragged them from under
his bed. He hurtled back downstairs and dropped
them at his feet. Then he rushed off and fetched
the newspaper.

Mr Marrow settled himself down in his armchair, and put his feet on the coffee table.

"Well, Patrick," he remarked. "It seems you really have managed to improve that mutt's abysmal behaviour. I only wish you could do something about that screaming brat. All your sister ever does is make an appalling noise, equally appalling smells - and dribble."

Patrick smiled mysteriously, but said nothing.

"The opposite of a noisy baby is a quiet baby," he murmured thoughtfully to himself. "I think Lizzy is about to get Reversing Peppermint Number Two."

If only things could have been that easy. But Patrick was in for quite a surprise, because his plan did not turn out anything like he expected!

CHAPTER FOUR

LIZZY

Patrick didn't get a chance to give Lizzy
a peppermint that evening, so the following morning
he woke up extra early and crept along the landing
to the little room at the end.
He pushed the door open, and peeped in.

As he expected, Lizzy was already wide awake.
She was standing at one end of her cot,
chewing the edge of a blanket.
She gurgled happily when she saw Patrick,
and waved a chubby pink hand at him.

"Gaa, Goo-oooooo, GAA-AAAAH," she chortled.

"Shut it, Slobber Chops!" hissed Patrick.
"Do you want everyone to hear you?"

He gave Lizzy a friendly pat on the head.
When she wasn't crying or wetting herself,
she was really rather cute,
and despite thinking babies were revolting,
Patrick had to admit he was very fond of her.

"The trouble is, you never stay this quiet
for long," he sighed. "But don't worry, you will
from now on. You'll be the quietest, cleanest
and best-behaved baby ever."

Patrick reached into his pyjama pocket and pulled
out the bag of Reversing Peppermints. He was just
about to hand one to Lizzy, when he remembered
the writing on the bag. He read it again,
especially the bit about babies being able to choke
on hard peppermints.

"You may be a noisy little pest," he said,
"But I certainly don't want you to choke."

He sat on the floor to think. Somehow, he would
have to dissolve the peppermint in her milk,
then feed it to her when she was ready
for her bottle. The problem was doing all this
without anyone catching him.

Before he could come up with a really good
fool-proof plan, the bedroom door opened
and Mrs Marrow bustled in.

"Oh, Patrick," she gasped. "You gave me
such a shock sitting there so quietly.
What on earth are you doing in here?"

"I came to see Lizzy," explained Patrick.
In an effort to sound convincing, he added,
"She's so adorable, I just love looking after her."

"Do you really?" replied Mrs Marrow doubtfully.
"Well, in that case you can do some baby-sitting
later this morning. I have to go across town,
to borrow your Aunt Susan's sewing machine.
Your father has a tear in his best suit,
and he needs it repairing before the interview
tomorrow morning."

"I hate baby-sitting," groaned Patrick.
"Babies are so jolly uncomfortable to sit on!"
Mrs Marrow laughed and gave her son a hug.

"You've just told me how much you enjoy looking
after her. I shall only be away for a couple
of hours. You can feed her, rock her to sleep
and, if necessary, you can change her as well."

Suddenly, Patrick had the most brilliant idea.
He'd change her, all right! While his mother
was out, he'd dissolve the peppermint in Lizzy's
bottle, and change her into the nicest little baby
imaginable.

"O.K.," he agreed. "Leave everything to me."

"Good boy," said Mrs Marrow. "Let's go downstairs.
The three of us can have an early breakfast,
before your father wakes up."

Before they went down, Patrick went to his room
to fetch Bouncer, but the dog's basket was empty.
When they reached the kitchen, they found him
hard at work trying to set the table.
Somehow, he had managed to open the cupboards
and carry the cups and plates and things
one at a time by holding them with his teeth.

Mrs Marrow could hardly believe her eyes.

"It's just like living with Lassie!" she gasped.
"But I shall have to wash the forks again,"
she explained to Patrick, "In case he held
the wrong ends in his mouth."

While she got busy, Bouncer ran to the front door
and picked up the Sunday newspaper,
which he carried upstairs and placed
on Mr Marrow's bedside table.

Then he came down with Mr Marrow's shoes
and left them by the back door ready to be
cleaned. Finally, he picked up his food bowl,
went to Mrs Marrow and sat up on his hind legs,
waiting patiently to be fed.

Breakfast was quite a pleasant meal
until Mr Marrow arrived. He stormed
into the kitchen and glared at everyone.

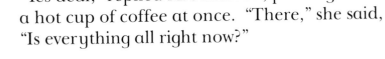

"What happened to
my early morning
coffee?" he thundered.
"You know how grouchy
I feel until I've had
my first cup."

"I'm so sorry dear,"
apologised Mrs Marrow.
"I thought Bouncer
had taken it up for you."
"Don't talk rot," Mr Marrow snarled.
"He's a dog, not a housemaid."

"Yes dear," replied Mrs Marrow, pouring him
a hot cup of coffee at once. "There," she said,
"Is everything all right now?"

"No, it is NOT!" came the reply. "I'm worried about the interview tomorrow. If I'm not promoted to the G.R.U.M.P. Co. board of directors, I'll never get to be a millionaire. And do you try to help me?!" he bellowed. "Do you BUMPKIN! You can't even cook me a decent breakfast!"

He slammed his fist on the table, making all the plates rattle. Patrick stared into his cup and said nothing, Lizzy began to cry and Mrs Marrow looked very sad and embarrassed.

"You don't deserve such a good husband!" roared Mr Marrow. "I'm off to the office now, to get my plans ready for tomorrow. When I get back, my best suit had better look like new, or there'll be trouble!"

He stamped out to his car and got in. With tyres screeching, it shot out of the gateway in a cloud of black smoke.

Lizzy started screaming louder than ever, and it took Mrs Marrow almost two hours to get her off to sleep.

At last she was ready to leave, so she put
Mr Marrow's best suit in a bag, and called Patrick
to give him his last minute instructions.

"I'm off to see your Aunt Susan now," she said.
"So I won't be back until later this afternoon.
Let Lizzy sleep as long as possible. She can have
her bottle when she wakes up. Make sure the milk
isn't too hot, and change her if she fills her nappy."

"I'll be changing her before that happens,"
thought Patrick to himself. But out loud he said,
"Don't worry. Everything will be fine."

Mrs Marrow took Bouncer with her for the walk,
so Patrick spent an enjoyable morning on his own
watching cartoons. Shortly after one o'clock,
Lizzy woke up and started making hungry noises,
so he switched the TV off,
and wandered into the kitchen.

He boiled milk in a pan, then dropped in
the peppermint and watched it dissolve.
After letting the mixture cool, he poured it
into Lizzy's bottle, and hurried upstairs.

By now, Lizzy's cries were quite deafening,
so Patrick wasted no time in shoving the teat
into her mouth. Instantly the crying ceased,
and all that could be heard was a gentle slurping
noise. Gradually the bottle emptied, and Lizzy lay
back in her cot with a contented smile on her face.

Patrick waited patiently for something to happen,
but to his dismay Lizzy began to whimper
and fidget.

"Perhaps she needs to get her wind up,"
he thought to himself.

So he picked Lizzy up, and started patting
her back, just as he had seen his mother do.

For a moment or two nothing happened, then at last
her tummy began to bumble and rumble and all of
a sudden she gave the most earth-shattering belch.

The force of it shot her right out
of Patrick's arms, and she flew backwards
round and round the room with bright yellow
smoke billowing out of her mouth.

Patrick wanted
to laugh.
She looked just
like a balloon
with all the air
wooshing out,
only instead of
getting smaller,
she seemed to be
growing larger
with every
passing
woosh.

After a couple of minutes she slowed down a little,
but then she gave another tremendous burp
and went zooming off again faster than ever,
right out of the open window!

She did seven loops of the chimney, then, with one
more enormous belch, she shot into the sky like
a rocket. Higher and higher she flew, until all
Patrick could see was a minute speck in the clouds.

Finally, the distant speck vanished,
and Patrick wondered if he would ever see
his baby sister again.

CHAPTER FIVE

GREAT AUNT ELIZABETH

Patrick stared
into the clouds
until his eyes ached.
Minutes ticked by
and still
there was no sign
of Lizzy.
Just as he was
about to give up,
the tiny speck
appeared once more
and grew larger
and larger as it
started to fall.

Patrick was by no means as relieved
as you may think. In fact, he was
in a complete state of panic, wondering
how on earth he would manage to catch her.

After all, having to tell your mother
that your sister had vanished into thin air
was one thing, but trying to explain
why she was splattered into a million bits
all over the front yard was quite another!

As Lizzy plummeted down, Patrick realized
the complete hopelessness of trying to catch her.

To begin with, she was at least several times larger than when she had shot up, and, secondly, the occasional little burp was still sending her spinning around all over the place.

All Patrick could do was stand and watch.

"She'll certainly make a fine mess of the flower beds," he thought to himself.

As she fell ever closer, Patrick could stand it no longer. He turned away from the window and shut his eyes. But he needn't have worried. As Lizzy came level with the house, she gave one last belch and shot towards the window.

There was however one minor problem. Being considerably larger than when she had left, she stuck in the window frame, like a cork in a bottle.

Whatever Patrick had **imagined** he would see when he finally opened his eyes, it did not come anywhere near the reality. For there in the window was the biggest, fattest old lady he had ever clapped eyes on!

"That was jolly good fun," she giggled. "Come on, Patrick. Stop gawping and pull me in. Half the town can see my bloomers."

Poor Patrick was still too shocked to move. As he looked closer, he saw there was a certain family resemblance about the old lady, and the awful truth dawned upon him.

The reverse of noisy may be quiet, but the reverse
of a baby was being old!

"You're Lizzy aren't you?" he gasped,
staring at her wrinkled face and silvery hair.

"Of course I am," she chuckled. "Get me inside,
quick, before mother comes home!"

Still in a daze, Patrick took hold of her gnarled,
wrinkled hands, and pulled with all his might.
His mind was in a whirl. However could he explain
to his mother why she now had a daughter
who was old enough to be her grandmother?
It was too confusing for words!

At first Lizzy seemed to be jammed solid, then all
at once she came loose and crashed to the floor
on top of poor Patrick. Before he could ask
if she was feeling all right, she had tottered
out of the bedroom door and down the stairs
into the kitchen.

"Now I've got some teeth at last,
I can start eating proper food, instead
of all that tasteless mush," laughed Lizzy,
as she opened the refrigerator door.
"Oooh, cheesecake! I can hardly wait!"
She settled herself down at the table, and tucked in.

"This **is** delicious. I always wondered
what it would taste like. I don't know how
you turned me into a grown-up, Patrick,
but I'm jolly glad you did!"

"It was the peppermint I gave you," said Patrick,
explaining how they turned people into the opposite
of whatever they were.

"But never mind about that," he went on,
with his head in his hands.
"What am I going to tell our parents?"

"Father wouldn't care if you'd turned me into
an elephant," said Lizzy, with her mouth full.

"Keep eating like that and you probably will turn into one," replied Patrick. "What will I say to mother?"

"You could tell her I'm her Great Aunt Elizabeth," suggested Lizzy. "Say that I've come here to stay with you."

"It might explain what you're doing here," Patrick agreed, "But she's still going to wonder where her baby has vanished to."

They both thought about it. Great Aunt Elizabeth thought so hard that she completely finished the cheesecake and devoured two packets of chocolate chip cookies.

"I know!" she gasped suddenly. "Give Mother one of the peppermints. Perhaps it will stop her being so motherly and she won't be bothered what's happened to her daughter."

"I like her just the way she is," said Patrick decidedly. "She's a kind and loving mother. It's Dad that needs reversing. It's his fault that Mother is always unhappy. He's so mean and horrible to her."

In the end, Patrick decided it would be best to act as if Lizzy was still around.
He found an enormous life-size baby doll someone had once bought for her, dressed it in her clothes and laid it in the cot.

The plan was that 'Great Aunt Elizabeth'
would pretend to look after the baby,
while trying to keep Mrs Marrow
from coming too close and seeing it was only a doll.

"I don't expect it will work for long,"
groaned Patrick. "But at least it will give us time
to think up a better plan."

Great Aunt Elizabeth went into the living room
with a huge bag of popcorn. Patrick was about
to follow when he glanced out of the window and saw
Mrs Marrow and Bouncer come through the gate,
and up the drive towards the house.

Bouncer walked without his leash,
but stayed close by Mrs Marrow's heels.
It was very unusual for him
not to be bounding around all over the place,
but Patrick had seen so many other peculiar
things that afternoon, he hardly noticed.

"How's my darling Lizzy?" called Mrs Marrow.

"She's been no trouble at all," replied Patrick
rather untruthfully.

"Did you manage to feed her all right?"

"Yes, thank you," replied Patrick, wondering
how he was going to explain about the cheesecake.
"She's back in her cot again now. Fast asleep."

"You've done very well," said his mother,
giving him a hug. "I'll just pop up and see her,
then I'll come right down and make dinner."

"Don't bother disturbing her," said Patrick,
wondering how to keep his mother downstairs.
Then he remembered. "We had a visitor
this afternoon. She's in the living room,
waiting to meet you."

"Why didn't you say so before?" said Mrs Marrow,
hanging her coat in the hall cupboard.
"Is it anyone we know?"

"In a way," laughed Patrick.
"She's a kind of relative."

Mrs Marrow hurried into the living room,
to find a large silvery-haired old lady
sprawled over the floor, flicking popcorn
between a pair of antique crystal vases.
"Goal!" she yelled. "Ten points for me!"

"What exactly is going on?" shrieked Mrs Marrow,
wondering if she was seeing things.

At the sound of her mother's voice, Lizzy almost
jumped out of her skin. She leapt nimbly to her
feet and mumbled, "Sorry, Mother." Then, suddenly
remembering the plan, she held out her hand
and said in her most grown-up voice, "Pleased to
meet you, my dear. I'm your Great Aunt Elizabeth."

"Pleased to meet you, too," replied Mrs Marrow politely. "May I ask what you were doing on the floor just now?"

"Patrick was trying to teach me one of his silly games," the old lady explained, giving her older (though much younger-looking) brother a nudge.

"Well, Patrick had better pick up every single bit of popcorn, and put my crystal vases back where he found them, or he'll be sent to bed without any dinner!" scolded Mrs Marrow.

Patrick knelt down and started to clear up, but not before he gave his younger (though much older-looking) sister his most furious glare.

"Will you be staying for dinner, Great Aunt Elizabeth?" Mrs Marrow asked her daughter.

"I'll be staying for longer than that," Lizzy replied. "I wrote last week to tell you that my house had been burnt down," she invented wildly. "And as you are my only living relatives, I explained that I was coming to live with you. Didn't you get my letter?"

"I don't think so," said Mrs Marrow unsurely. "But make yourself at home, and I'll make dinner."

She hurried along the hall to the kitchen in a complete daze, wondering what on earth her husband would say when he discovered they had a new member of the family.

She didn't have long to wait.
Seconds later,
he burst in through the door,
yelling, "I'M HOME!"
as loudly as ever.
"I hope you've got
the dinner ready,"
he said to his wife,
as he took his slippers
and newspaper
from the efficient
Bouncer.

"Not quite, dear," apologised Mrs Marrow.
"I'm afraid something has happened,
and I've been rather held up."

"Don't tell me all the potatoes escaped again,"
sneered Mr Marrow sarcastically.
"Or did the vacuum cleaner try to attack you
when you pulled it out of the hall cupboard?"

Mrs Marrow said nothing. She did not appreciate
her husband's sarcastic sense of humour.
She gave a deep sigh, explained about Great Aunt
Elizabeth and started getting the dinner ready.

Dinner was a dismal meal. Mr Marrow decided
he did not like Great Aunt Elizabeth at all,

because she was far too busy eating
to be interested in his plans for invisible smog.

"You see," he explained. " If the smog
is invisible, no one will be able to see all
the pollution made by our factories."

"Wouldn't it be better if you stopped making
pollution altogether?" enquired Patrick.

"Shut up, you ignorant little toad!" thundered
his father. "Pollution makes money. I've been
making pollution since your bottom was as big
as a shirt button. But up to now, people have been
able to see it. Once it's invisible, they won't
even know it's there, so they can't blame
G.R.U.M.P. Co. for making them cough. If that
doesn't get me a place on the board of directors,
I'll eat one of Bouncer's old bones."

Patrick was horrified. He was now completely
convinced that his father was thoroughly selfish
and unpleasant and needed teaching a lesson.
He decided there and then that it was time to use
the next Reversing Peppermint, despite the trouble
they had already caused.

"It can't make things any worse," thought Patrick
to himself.

Perhaps that was true.

On the other hand,
perhaps it wasn't...

CHAPTER SIX

MRS MARROW

Patrick wondered if he could manage to slip
a peppermint into his father's hot drink,
without anyone noticing. But the peppermints
always seemed to have such spectacular effects.
He would have an awful lot of explaining to do
if his mother saw her husband zooming around the
kitchen with blue smoke pouring out of his ears.

It was obvious to Patrick that he would have
to think things out very carefully. For his plan
to work properly, his father would have to eat
the peppermint alone, yet before his interview
the following morning. The problem was, he wouldn't
be alone all evening, and breakfast time
would be just as awkward as dinner time.

He sat back in his chair and thought hard
while Bouncer cleared the plates away
and dropped them one at a time into the sink.

"Dessert, anyone?" asked Mrs Marrow.

"Oooh, yes, please, Mother!" said Great Aunt
Elizabeth excitedly.

Everyone stared, and Patrick kicked her under
the table. Great Aunt Elizabeth tried to kick
back, but missed and kicked her father instead.

Mr Marrow was furious. "You may be my Great Aunt Whatz-er-name," he snarled, "but do that once more and I'll creep into your room at midnight and stick a frog in your bloomers!"

Lizzy was determined to get her own back, so when Mrs Marrow discovered that the cheesecake was missing, she said that Patrick had eaten it.

"I DID NOT!" cried Patrick, kicking her again. But this time, his mother caught him in the act.

"You wicked boy!" she exclaimed. "First you steal the dessert, then you lie about it, and worst of all you kick a poor defenceless old lady. Go up to your room this instant!"

Patrick walked out of the room and up the stairs, secretly quite glad to get out of the kitchen.

"Defenceless old lady indeed," he laughed. "They wouldn't say that if they'd seen her zooming around the chimney."

Now that he had some peace and quiet, he sat on the end of his bed and tried hard to think of a way to give his father a peppermint. He drew his feet up onto the bed and rested his chin on his knees. Suddenly he had the most brilliant flash of inspiration. He knew what suit his father was wearing tomorrow, because his mother had repaired it and hung it on the back of their bedroom door. All he had to do

was to slip the peppermint into one of the pockets.
Mr Marrow was bound to
find it and eat it
before he arrived
at the office.

Patrick took
the paper bag
out of his pocket
and rummaged in it
for Peppermint
Number Three.
Then he sneaked
along the landing
to his parents' room
and slipped it
in the right hand
pocket of his father's
best suit.

Meanwhile, Lizzy was feeling guilty about getting
Patrick in trouble. But that wasn't all.
She had a nasty feeling that she was only minutes
away from disaster.

Mrs Marrow had just prepared some mushed-up
baby food, and was about to go upstairs.
Somehow, she had to be stopped.

"Fancy my little Lizzy sleeping
right through dinner," Mrs Marrow remarked
to Great Aunt Elizabeth. "I've been so flustered
I quite forgot to wake her."

"I expect that's my fault," confessed the old lady.
Then, remembering Patrick's plan, she said,
"You look ever so tired, my dear.
Why don't you have an early night?
I can feed Lizzy for you."

"Are you sure you can manage?" asked Mrs Marrow,
doubtfully.

"No problem at all, dearie," came the reply.
"You don't get to my age without knowing a thing
or two about babies. I'll even change her, and
settle her back in her cot. You have a good rest
and you'll feel a different woman in the morning."

Mrs Marrow was very grateful. She hadn't had
an early night for years, so she went straight
upstairs to her room. She took off her stained
old apron, crumpled clothes and laddered tights,
brushed her straggly hair and gazed at her tired,
worn face in the mirror.

"If only my husband realised what a full time job housework is," she sighed. "I sometimes wish I could work in an office. At least I could get dressed nicely for a change."

She staggered into the bathroom, showered, and brushed her teeth, and in no time at all, she was ready for bed.

She wanted to say 'Good Night' to Lizzy, but Great Aunt Elizabeth was just coming out of her room and said that she had already gone back to sleep.

Next, she said a rather frosty 'Good Night' to Patrick, telling him to behave better in future. Finally, she went downstairs to say 'Good Night' to her husband.

"I hope everything goes well for you tomorrow, dear," she said to him, though, to be perfectly honest, she had no interest whatsoever in business matters.

"It will, if you remember my early morning coffee," snapped Mr Marrow. "You can wake me up half an hour earlier than usual," he added. "And don't forget to put a clean white handkerchief in my suit pocket."

Mrs Marrow promised to do everything. As a special treat, she made herself a hot drink of cocoa and went up to her room. She was just about to climb into bed when she remembered the instructions about

the clean white handkerchief,
so she fetched one from the closet and slipped it
into the pocket of Mr Marrow's best suit.

To her surprise, she felt something small and hard
at the bottom of the pocket; something she hadn't
noticed when she had repaired the suit earlier.
Full of curiosity, she pulled it out. When she saw
it was a peppermint she could hardly believe her
eyes. The last time Mr Marrow had bought her
any peppermints had been before they were even
married. Unable to resist, she unwrapped
the shiny, blue paper and popped the peppermint
into her mouth.

It was delicious.
The best peppermint
she had ever tasted.
She lay in bed,
savouring every
single chew. After
drinking her cocoa,
she turned out
the light and sank
into the deepest
and most contented
sleep imaginable.

While she slept, Mrs Marrow floated silently
around the bedroom, her gentle snoring sounds
sending tiny wisps of blue smoke wafting out
of her nostrils. Finally, the blue smoke faded
and she sank softly back onto the bed.

Just as Great Aunt Elizabeth had promised,
Mrs Marrow would feel a different woman
in the morning!

CHAPTER SEVEN

MISS KARRINGTON

Patrick lay in bed, trying to imagine
what would happen to his father
when he ate the Third Peppermint.

At first he wondered if it would reverse his age,
as it had done with Lizzy. But after some thought
he decided it probably wouldn't, because both his
parents were middle-aged, which didn't seem to have
an opposite. Finally he gave up and went to sleep,
content to see what tomorrow would bring.

The following day brought many surprises,
and the first three were in the form of short,
hand-written notes left on three bedside tables.

The note that Patrick found said this:-

Dear Patrick,

I left the house extra early this morning.
Please make your own breakfast and get to school
on time. See you later.

Your loving Mother.

The note that Lizzy found said this:-

> **Dear Great Aunt Elizabeth,**
>
> **I shall be out all day.**
> **Please would you take care of Lizzy for me?**
> **See you this evening.**
>
> **Your loving Niece.**

The note that Mr Marrow found said this:-

> **Dear Mostyn,**
>
> **I am sick and tired of being your slave.**
> **I have gone out to get myself a job.**
> **I hope you have a rotten day. See you soon!**
>
> **Most sincerely, Angela.**

Mr Marrow pinched himself to see
if he was still dreaming, but to his great dismay
he discovered that things were horribly real!

He read the note a second time
and scratched his head,
wondering who was going to make his breakfast.
Then, as he put
the note back
on the
bedside table,
he saw the hands
of the clock
pointing to
five minutes
to nine.

"I've overslept!" he gasped.
"The most important day of my life and I'm going
to be late! What on earth will Mr Griswald say?"

The G.R.U.M.P. Co, office block opened its doors
at nine o'clock sharp, and Mr Marrow was due
to have his interview at fifteen minutes past.
There was no time for him to have breakfast now,
so he jumped out of bed and got dressed,
without even bothering to wash or shave himself.
But so great was his hurry, he failed to notice

that his best suit had been swapped
for his gardening clothes.
They were old, muddy and a little too small.

He rushed downstairs and snatched a cup of coffee
out of Great Aunt Elizabeth's hand.
Without even bothering to say goodbye, he leapt
into his car and zoomed off, trying to sip it,
as he drove through the traffic jams.

By the time he arrived at the office
it was already twenty minutes to eleven.
He had coffee stains all over his clean white shirt
and looked more like a tramp than an executive.

He stepped into the elevator,
and pressed the top button, which would take him
to Mr Griswald's Executive Suite.
When the elevator doors opened,
he hurried along the corridor to the board room.
Miss Guffin, Mr Griswald's personal secretary,
sat at her desk, just outside the boardroom door.
She peered at Mr Marrow critically.

"Name?" she asked in an icy voice.

"Mostyn Marrow," replied Mr Marrow nervously.

"You're late," remarked Miss Guffin, consulting
her appointment book. "You'll have to wait.
Mr Griswald is interviewing someone else."

Mr Marrow was astonished. He had thought
he was the only person being considered for a place
on the Board of Directors.

"Who is he?" he snarled suspiciously.

"It isn't a HE, it's a SHE," said Miss Guffin
frostily. "Her name is Miss Karrington,
and she looks considerably more efficient than you."

Mr Marrow could hardly believe it. He flopped
into a chair and put his head in his hands,
feeling terribly confused. Try as he might,
he could not think of anyone called Karrington
in the entire G.R.U.M.P. Co. building.
Yet, for some peculiar reason, the name sounded
vaguely familiar. It was very odd indeed!

Poor Mr Marrow waited for what seemed like hours, though it was in fact only about forty-five minutes. At last, the board room door crashed open and a booming voice called, "IS MARROW HERE YET?" "Yes," replied Miss Guffin.

"WELL, SEND HIM IN!" the voice boomed.

Mr Marrow leapt to his feet, and scurried towards the door. As he hurried in, an elegantly dressed lady, wearing a wide-brimmed hat, stepped out and passed him. He had a strange feeling that he had met her before, but before he could remember where, the booming voice thundered, "GET A MOVE ON MARROW, WE HAVEN'T GOT ALL DAY!"

Mr Griswald presided at the head of a long, narrow table, which had company directors sitting all the way down either side. Mr Marrow was motioned to an empty chair at the foot of the table. He sat down and cleared his throat.

"WELL?" roared Griswald.

At that very moment, Mostyn Marrow remembered something that sent an icy chill down his spine, while simultaneously making him blush as red as a strawberry. In his haste, he had forgotten to bring his briefcase, containing all his plans for invisible smog!

He muttered and spluttered, desperately trying to bluff his way through the interview, but he was doomed from the start.

"INVISIBLE SMOG," snarled Mr Griswald. "Is that it?"

Mr Marrow nodded silently.

"What this company needs is someone with vision and foresight," Mr Griswald continued. "Someone with bold, new ideas and courageous concepts who can give G.R.U.M.P. Co, a brand new image. For the last two years I have been searching for someone to replace me when I retire, and today, finally, I have met that person."

"That's me!" thought Mr Marrow to himself, as Mr Griswald walked towards him with his right hand held out.

He tried to look modest, but failed dismally.

But instead of shaking Mr Marrow by the hand, Mr Griswald walked right past him, and opened the boardroom door. In strolled Miss Karrington, as all the executives clapped and cheered.

"At last I have found someone
who will run this company
without causing any pollution at all,"
announced Mr Griswald, as he escorted
Miss Karrington to his chair at the head
of the table. "I shall retire today,"
he continued, "And from now on
this company will be known as K.O.F.Co.,
Karrington's Ozone Friendly Company."

Everyone cheered. Well, almost everyone.

Mr Marrow sat in silence with a face like thunder,
as Miss Karrington removed her wide-brimmed hat.
He had just remembered that Angela Karrington
had been his wife's name before they were married.
And now that he could see her face for the first time,
he realised that Miss Karrington was, in fact,
Mrs Marrow!

He was too shocked to speak.

"Thank you, fellow board members," boomed Miss Karrington. "Over the next few days I intend to make several changes in the way this company is run. However," she added, "My first and most enjoyable job will be to get rid of that nauseating little worm at the other end of the table."

"MOSTYN MARROW, YOU'RE FIRED!"

Poor Mr Marrow staggered out of the boardroom in a complete state of shock.

"Hand your company car keys to Miss Guffin before you leave," shouted his wife.
"From now on, that will be her car."

As if in a dream, Mr Marrow did as he was told. Wondering if things could possibly get any worse, he pressed the button for the elevator.

"The elevator is for employees' use only," smiled Miss Guffin. "**You'll** have to use the stairs!"

CHAPTER EIGHT

MISS BUNION

Patrick was having a miserable morning.
Ever since his class had got a new teacher,
he had absolutely hated going to school.

Her name was Miss Bunion and she did not like
being a teacher. To be perfectly honest,
Miss Bunion did not even like children,
and a teacher who does not like children
is about as much use as a poke in the eye.
Both her parents had been teachers,
and they insisted that she became one too.
Miss Bunion had wanted to go to Egypt
to look for a mummy in the pyramids,
but she didn't have enough money.
"I'll be a teacher until I've saved up,"
she decided. But by the time she had earned
her fare, she was rather old and had to look after
her own mummy who was ill in bed. That made
her cross and mean with everyone, but especially
with children who forgot to do their homework.

Patrick was always forgetting to do his homework,
but for once in his life he had a good excuse.
But turning his sister into an old lady was not the
sort of excuse a teacher like Miss Bunion would
ever believe, even though it happened to be true.

Miss Bunion glared at him over the tops of her gold
rimmed spectacles.
"Without any doubt," she hissed.
"You are the most deceitful little toad
I have ever had the misfortune to teach."

"And you," thought Patrick
to himself, "are the ugliest old cabbage
I have ever clapped eyes on!"

To be perfectly honest, she was.

Her gingery hair
had been scraped
back into
a tiny bun,
which was fixed
to the back
of her scalp
with a mass
of hairpins.
She had a long
pointed nose,
a chin covered
in little hairy moles,
and eyes that were
small and dark,
with a mean glint in them.
But worst of all, she smelt funny!

For some peculiar reason, Miss Bunion always
seemed to smell of onions.
In fact the very first day she taught her new class,

she was secretly given the nickname
'Bunion the Onion', because she was smelly
and liked to make people cry!

All morning she scolded Patrick
every time he got something wrong, and every time
he got something right she accused him of cheating.
First thing after lunch, she told the class
to get out their exercise books,
as she was going to give them a test
on the things they should have learnt that weekend.

"The brainless little noggin who comes bottom,
will stay behind after school,"
she said looking directly at Patrick.
"And, as a punishment, he can run fifty times round
the school yard."

Patrick was furious. He felt sure that Miss Bunion
was giving the test on purpose to catch him out.
So it looked as if he'd be staying behind
after school, which was especially annoying
when he could hardly wait to get home and find out
what had happened to his father.

"If only I could be a child genius, instead
of an utter dunce," Patrick thought to himself.
He wasn't a dunce really, but he wasn't exactly top
of the class either! Then suddenly he realised:
dunce and genius were opposites! All he had to do
was take one of his own Reversing Peppermints,
and he'd be top of the class every single time.

Like most teachers, Miss Bunion had lots
of silly rules, such as, 'No Looking
Out Of The Window', or, 'No Borrowing Your Best
Friend's Purple Crayon.' But the rule she kept
most strictly of all, was 'No Eating Sweets During
Lessons'!

As quiet as a mouse, Patrick rummaged around
in his pocket until he found the peppermint
with Number Four printed on its shiny green paper.
Then he pulled it out, and tried to unwrap it
silently under his desk.

Now, some people will try to tell you that NOTHING
is impossible. But as it so happens, there are
three things in this world that ARE impossible.

Firstly, it is impossible for a worm to fall over.
Secondly, it is impossible to pick your nose while
wearing mittens. And thirdly,
and perhaps most important to remember,
it is impossible to unwrap shiny paper
off a really sticky peppermint without making
a noise!

Patrick soon discovered this for himself.
No matter how slowly and carefully he tried to peel
back the shiny paper, it crackled all the more.

"WHO IS TRYING TO UNWRAP A SWEET?!"
bellowed Miss Bunion. The class remained silent
and put on their most innocent expressions.

"HANDS UP! EVERYONE!" she thundered.

Every pupil put both hands in the air,
and every single hand was empty. This was exactly
what Bunion the Onion had expected.
She was an expert at catching sweet unwrappers.

"Now I've caught you," she hissed,
in a dangerously quiet voice.
"One of you revolting little maggots has a sweet
balanced on your knee - I can smell it.
So when I count three, you can all stand up.

One - TWO - **THREE!**"

The entire class stood up, and the peppermint
that Patrick had wedged between his knee
and the desk clattered to the floor by his feet.

"YOU!!!" roared Miss Bunion.
"I should have guessed. Bring that peppermint
to the front and put it on my desk."

Reluctantly, Patrick did as he was told.

"Now climb on your chair and stand on one leg,"
ordered Miss Bunion, extracting something
long and sharp from the back of her gingery bun.

"You can stay like that for the rest
of the afternoon," she explained.
"And every time you wobble
I will spike your bottom with my hairpin!"

Patrick tried
his hardest
not to wobble,
but about
five minutes
before the end
of the lesson,
his leg went numb
and he started
wobbling about all over the place.
His bottom got so spiked that he felt as if he'd sat
on a hedgehog!

As soon as the school bell rang,
Patrick leapt off his chair, snatched his bag
and headed for the door.

"And where do you think you're going?"
asked Miss Bunion, grabbing him by the collar.

"Home," said Patrick. "Like everyone else."

"But you came bottom in the test," she snarled.

I didn't even take the test," gasped Patrick.
"I was standing on my chair the whole time."

"Precisely," said Miss Bunion with a sinister smile.
"Zero out of twenty. Get running round

the school yard. Fifty laps before you go home.
I'll be watching you through the window."

Patrick could hardly believe it.
He gave a huge sigh and started running,
slowly at first because his leg was still numb.

In the classroom, Miss Bunion looked at her watch.

"Ten minutes," she groaned.
"And he's only done five and a half laps.
I'll be here for ages."

Most teachers would have let Patrick off,
and gone home. But Bunion the Onion
took her punishments very seriously.
She looked around the classroom,
wondering what she could do to pass the time.

Suddenly something on the desk caught her eye;
something small and green, but very shiny.
For a moment she couldn't think what it was,
then all at once she remembered.
It was the peppermint.
Slowly she unwrapped it, making as much noise
as she wanted, then with a huge grin,
popped it into her mouth.

Patrick was just starting his sixth lap
of the school yard when he heard the sound
of breaking glass.
He glanced over his shoulder and saw something
zooming out of his classroom window,
with bright green smoke streaming out behind.

"Oh, no!" he panted.
"It's the world's first jet-propelled teacher."
He watched with horror as Miss Bunion
did seven super-fast spirals, then off she shot
like a rocket. Higher and higher she went,
until she vanished into the clouds.

"Not again!" groaned Patrick.
Then, realising this was his chance to escape,
he dashed out of the school gates and ran home,
before Bunion the Onion came back down to earth!

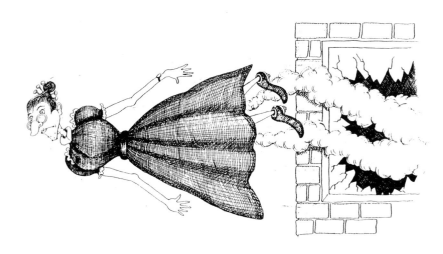

CHAPTER NINE

MR MARROW

Patrick was not the only one to be having his share of troubles that day. In fact Mr Marrow was having considerably more than his share.

He had left G.R.U.M.P. Co.,
or K.O.F.Co., as it was now called,
at about half past twelve.
As he had no car
to drive,
he headed for
the nearest
bus stop. Then,
he discovered
that his pockets
were empty
and his wallet
was still
in his best suit
back at home,
so he had no money
for the fare.
Poor Mr Marrow!
He had no choice.
He took a deep breath
and set off
on the longest walk of his life.

Later that afternoon, while Mr Marrow
was still plodding along, his son was running;
out of the school gate and home.

Patrick kept on going
until he reached
the corner
of his street.
Then he leaned back
against a lamp post
and tried
to catch his breath.

In his hurry he had left his bag behind
in the school yard. It had his homework inside,
but he was far too tired to go back and get it.

"Never mind," he thought to himself.
"Perhaps the peppermint has reversed Miss Bunion
into a **really nice** teacher. Then she won't mind
whether I do my homework or not."

Patrick looked at his watch.
"Dad should be home any minute now," he chuckled
to himself. "I wonder how he got on with
the interview after eating his peppermint.
If it worked properly,
he should be quite a different person by now."

As he turned in through the gate and walked
up the drive towards the house, a huge midnight –
blue limousine swept past him, sounding its horn.

"Looks like he got his place on the board
of directors after all," thought Patrick, rather puzzled.
"And he's got a brand new car to prove it."

But when the car door opened,
Patrick got the surprise of his life.

"MOTHER!" he gasped. "Is it really you?"

"Yes, Patrick," she replied. "It is me.
I seem to have woken up this morning an entirely
different person. So I applied for the same job
that your father had an interview for.
Not only did I beat him, but I am now the Managing
Director of my very own company."

"Congratulations!" said Patrick.
"What did Father say?"

"Nothing!" laughed Mrs Marrow.
"I fired him before he had a chance to open
his mouth. I expect he's home already."

But as it had turned out, the house was completely
empty, and all Mrs Marrow found was a note
on the kitchen table:

i hav gon owt too the play grownd.
i wil be bak in tim for dinna.
grate ant Elizzybiff.

"What very odd spelling!" remarked Mrs Marrow.

"She never went to school," explained Patrick truthfully.
"I'm surprised her writing is as good as that."

"Well, I hope she isn't letting Lizzy go on the swings or slide," said his mother anxiously.
"She's not old enough."

"Perhaps she just took her out in the pram, for a walk," suggested Patrick.
"Would you like me to run down to the park and see if I can find them?"

"Oh, yes," said Mrs Marrow gratefully.
"You hurry along, and I'll have dinner ready when the three of you get back."

When Patrick got to the playground, he found his elderly looking sister with tears pouring down her cheeks.

"Oh, Patrick," she wept. "I am glad to see you."

"What's up, Lizzy?" asked Patrick.

"I got so bored left on my own all day,
I decided to come to the playground and have
some fun," she sniffed. "I brought the baby doll
out in the pram, in case Mother came home.
I even left her a note. Then, just a couple
of minutes ago, while I was on the roundabout,
a girl with long, red hair and glasses came,
stole the doll and ran off. Now, I don't know
what to do. That doll was the only thing
that kept Mother from suspecting the truth."

"Never mind," said Patrick.
"We tricked Mother last night,
but we'd never manage to fool her a second time.
We've got to think of a more permanent solution
to the problem."

"Couldn't you find another real baby instead?"
asked Lizzy.
"Babies don't grow on trees," replied Patrick,
shuddering at the thought. "And even if I could
get a replacement baby from somewhere,
I'm sure mother would be able to tell."

"I wish **I** was a baby again," groaned Lizzy.
"Being grown up isn't as much fun as I thought."

"The warning on the peppermint paper
said the effects were permanent
and wouldn't wear off," sighed Patrick.

"Isn't there **something** you can do?" begged Lizzy.

"Perhaps there is," replied Patrick thoughtfully.
"But the only person who would know is Dr Tapioca
himself. I'll go to the market again tomorrow, on
my way home from school, and see if I can find him.

Meanwhile we'll tell Mother that you took Lizzy
to visit Aunt Susan, and left her there.
I don't think she'll be too bothered. She's changed.
She must have eaten the peppermint
I put in Dad's suit pocket, because she hardly
seems like our mother at all!"

They walked home together, pushing
the empty pram and rehearsing their story.

"She fell asleep while Susan was holding her,"
Great Aunt Elizabeth explained to her mother.
"It seemed such a pity to wake her, so Susan said
that she'd look after her for the night, and
I'll pick her up again first thing in the morning."

"As it happens, I'm rather glad," confided
Mrs Marrow. "Ever since I woke up this morning,
things have seemed different. Now I feel my career
is far more important than a baby.
I'm glad the little nuisance is out of the house,
so I can get on with all the paperwork I brought
home from the office, without being disturbed."

Then the three of them had dinner.
It was only bread and butter followed by a bowl
of ice-cream, because Mrs Marrow said that 'top
business executives were far too busy to prepare
meals'. However, she did decide to phone
Aunt Susan to check that Lizzy was all right,
but Patrick had secretly cut the telephone wires,
so she asked him to call in at Aunt Susan's
when he took Bouncer out for his walk later.

Just then, the front door swung open
and in staggered Mr Marrow,
looking as if he were about to collapse.

"Fetch my slippers," he groaned.
"My feet are killing me. I hope dinner's ready.
I'm absolutely starving."

"You can fetch your own slippers,"
replied Mrs Marrow with a scornful smile.
"And when you come down your dinner
will be on the table. And make the most of it,"
she added. "Because it's the last meal
I'll ever be making for you."

Mr Marrow couldn't believe his ears.

"Things couldn't get any worse than this,"
he thought to himself. But when he got
into the kitchen he found out that they could.
There on the kitchen table sat
a huge, smelly, raw bone.

"You said you'd eat one of Bouncer's old bones
if you didn't get a place on the board
of directors," laughed Mrs Marrow.
"I hope you enjoy it. I dug it up especially!"

Mr Marrow fainted, and to bring him round,
Mrs Marrow emptied the cold washing up water
over his head.

"From now on YOU can cook the meals,"
she told him. "And while I'm out at the office,
you can care for Lizzy, do the shopping,
the cleaning, the dusting, the vacuuming,
the laundry and all the gardening.
Then we'll see if you **STILL** think housework
isn't a proper job!"

"I'm a business executive, not a housemaid,"
gasped Mr Marrow in disbelief.
"I couldn't possibly change."

"You'll have to!" snapped Mrs Marrow.
"I did, and so can you."

Then she stormed out of the kitchen,
slamming the door behind her.

"People can't turn into the complete opposite
of what they are," wept Mr Marrow.
"It's impossible."

"Oh yes they can," thought Patrick to himself.
"Cheer up Dad," he said.
"Here, have a peppermint!"

CHAPTER TEN

MOSTYN

Mr Marrow took the peppermint with the number five printed on its shiny orange paper, unwrapped it, and tossed it into his mouth.

"Any second now!" thought Patrick to himself, seeing the first wisps of orange smoke hovering beneath his father's nostrils. He locked the kitchen door, pulled down the blinds and crawled under the table. By now, he knew what kind of effect the peppermints had, and in such an enclosed space, guessed he would need somewhere to shelter.

He was right. Mr Marrow launched off his chair and smashed into the ceiling. With bright orange smoke spluttering out of his nose, he zoomed around the kitchen, crashing into the walls, colliding with the cupboards and bouncing off the floor. Patrick sat safely under the table, unable to see much through the thick smoke.

Finally, Mr Marrow seemed to stop, and Patrick
opened the windows to let the smoke out.
When at last he was able to see clearly,
he gasped with horror. The room looked as if
it had been struck by a whirlwind, a flash-flood
and an earthquake, all at once. His father
was slumped in the sink, covered in bumps
and bruises. There was a huge egg-shaped lump
on the top of his head, a vacant look in his eyes
and he grinned stupidly from ear to ear.
Patrick was terrified in case any permanent harm
had been done, but there were only
a few small cracks in the ceiling.

Mr Marrow gazed round the kitchen,
then shook himself.

"My, what a mess!"
he exclaimed.
"I'd better get busy
tidying it up at once."
Then he leapt out
of the sink
and put on an apron
and a pair of pink
rubber gloves.
In no time at all
he was scrubbing,
washing, dusting
and polishing,
until the kitchen
shone like a new pin.

It was almost midnight when he had everything
tidied to his satisfaction. He was just hanging up
his apron, when the door burst open and Mrs Marrow
marched in. She stared in astonishment
at his bruised appearance.

"Have you been attacked by the feather duster?"
she sneered sarcastically. "While you've been
playing house, I've been doing some proper work,
so now I'm off to bed. Don't forget to wake me
at seven-thirty with my early morning coffee.
And I want a full cooked breakfast tomorrow,
before I leave for the office."

"Yes, dear," said Mr Marrow meekly.
"Leave everything to me."

As Patrick ate his toast the following morning,
it occurred to him that his family were now
the complete opposite of what they had been
on Saturday. It was just as he had wished, but for
some odd reason, things seemed strangely familiar.

He glanced across the table at his mother,
whose eyes were devouring the Financial Times
faster than her mouth could devour her breakfast,
and at his father who bustled around in an apron,
serving porridge and scrambled eggs
to his geriatric daughter.

Mrs Marrow drank the last of her coffee
and stood up.

"I'm off to the office," she announced, brushing
toast crumbs off her immaculate business suit.
"And when I get back, this house had better be
spotless, Mostyn. Or there'll be trouble!"
She marched out of the house, slamming the door
behind her.

Mr Marrow gave a deep sigh and began washing
the dishes.

"Come along Patrick, you'll be late for school,"
he fussed. Then, turning to Great Aunt Elizabeth,
he said, "Don't forget to fetch Lizzy this morning.
I do miss the little sweetie, I can hardly wait
to have her back home."

Things were no better than they had been last week,
and in some ways they were worse!

"This is serious. We've got to do something about
Lizzy, er... I mean YOU," Patrick whispered
to his sister, feeling a little muddled.
"If Dad doesn't see you, as a baby, back
in your cot by lunch time, he'll get suspicious.
You'll have to go to the market yourself
and look for Dr Tapioca, and see if he can help."

Lizzy nodded. Patrick glanced hurriedly
at his watch, then shot out of the house, groaning,
"Oh, no! I'm going to be late again!"

When Patrick had gone, Mr Marrow went upstairs to make the beds and tidy the bathroom.
Lizzy went into the living room and switched on the television. It was time for her favourite programme – "Play Bus". She usually watched it, sitting on her mum's lap, but as she was alone, she sprawled on the floor with her thumb in her mouth.

"Let's pretend to be circus animals," smiled the lady on the television.
"First, we are going to be elephants."

Lizzy stood up and lumbered around the room, using one arm as a trunk.

"Next, we are going to be lions," continued the lady.

Lizzy crouched on all fours and roared as loud as she could. Upstairs, Mr Marrow leapt out of his skin and hurried down to see what was happening.

"Now you can be any animal you like," said the lady.

Lizzy decided to be a kangaroo, so she started bounding round the room, shouting "Boing!" every time she jumped. She was just leaping back and forward over the coffee table when Mr Marrow burst in.

"What ARE you doing?" he screeched.

"I'm a kangaroo," she shouted breathlessly.
"Boing, boing, boing!" Then suddenly she realised
that she was meant to be a frail old lady,
so she stopped 'Boinging' and flopped into a chair.

"You're most certainly not a kangaroo,"
gasped Mr Marrow. "You are not Great Aunt
Elizabeth either," he continued. "I suspect
you are an imposter."

Lizzy sat very still and looked worried.
"You say that you've come to live with us,
so where are all your suitcases?" roared Mr Marrow.
"And what's more," he went on. "I've just looked
through our old family album, and we don't have
a Great Aunt Elizabeth. What have you got to say
about that?"

Lizzy said nothing.

"You didn't sleep in the spare bedroom last night, did you?" he shouted. "No, you slept in Lizzy's cot. And I think you cut the telephone wires last night as well."

Lizzy was horrified. There was nothing for it but to tell the truth. "I'm your daughter," she whispered.

"YOU ARE A COMPLETE LUNATIC!" yelled Mr Marrow.
"And what is more, I think you have kidnapped my daughter. You have until noon to fetch her back, or I shall go next door and 'phone the police."

Lizzy ran out of the house with tears streaming down her face. She hurried along the streets to the centre of town, and spent the entire morning searching for Dr Tapioca at the market.
But there was no one there fitting the description that Patrick had given her, and what was more, none of the other stall holders had ever heard of him.
Finally, she had no choice but to give up.
She trudged miserably home, wondering what it would be like being arrested and put in prison.

Poor Lizzy racked her brains trying to come up with a plan that would somehow make everything all right, but in the end she had to admit that she was beaten.

Meanwhile, Mr Marrow had spent a busy morning
spring-cleaning the house from top to bottom.
Lizzy walked in through the front door
and found him in the living room,
taking down the curtains to be washed.

"Well, where is my daughter?" he demanded.

"I've told you," sighed Lizzy.
"**I'M** your daughter."

"Trying to plead insanity, eh?" laughed Mr Marrow,
turning to leave. "That won't work.
I'm off to 'phone the police."

Lizzy was frantic. She simply HAD to do something.

"Please don't do that," she wept. Then, throwing
herself at his feet, she grabbed hold of his legs
in an attempt to stop him.

Mr Marrow tried to move, but he couldn't.
Suddenly over-balancing, he slumped to the floor
like a sack of old potatoes. He whacked his head
on the brass umbrella stand, giving him another
large egg-shaped lump. In a trice, Lizzy grabbed
the curtains, and trussed up her unconscious father
like a chicken.

She was only just in time.
Seconds later he came round and began to struggle.
Mr Marrow was furious. He started shouting for
help, but Lizzy gagged him with a cushion cover
and shut him in the hall cupboard.

"That's turned the tables!" exclaimed Lizzy.
"Let's see how YOU like being blamed for something
you haven't done."

She fetched some paper and a pencil, and began
to write. When she had finished, she took the note
upstairs and placed it in the cot. It said:

i hav kidnapt yor dorter
if yoo want hur bak, then
make me a cumpany direktor.

yors threatingly,
 Mostin marrow

P.S. if you fone the poliss
you will never see hur aggen!

CHAPTER ELEVEN

AMMONIA

Meanwhile, Patrick had been having
a most unusual morning at school. He **was** late.
But, as it happened, Miss Bunion was late too,
so he had time to find his bag, and creep
into the classroom without getting caught.

It wasn't until he sat at his desk,
that he remembered about Miss Bunion
eating the peppermint and flying out of the window
in a cloud of green smoke.

"I suppose that's why she's late this morning,"
he thought to himself. "Probably the opposite
of a strict, punctual teacher, is a kind teacher
who is always late."

But Miss Bunion wasn't late.
She was already in the classroom. She had changed
so much that Patrick didn't even recognise her.

Twenty minutes later, there was still no sign
of a teacher and the class were beginning to enjoy
themselves. Paper planes zoomed to and fro
and bits of pencil-eraser and bubble gum were
flicked off the ends of rulers. It was all pretty
harmless and lots of fun, but one girl decided
it was not enough. She had gingery plaits,
large round glasses and freckles.

"Who wants
to see me
get up to
some really
SUPER mischief?"
she asked,
standing on
Miss Bunion's desk.
A few of the naughtier pupils did,
so they put their hands up and cheered.

"Is that all?" squealed the girl.
"What about you Patrick? Don't you want to see
some REAL fun?"

Patrick was astonished. He had never seen the girl
before and wondered how she knew his name.

"Who are you?" he asked. "Are you new here?"

"No," giggled the girl. "I just look different.
My name is Ammonia – Ammonia BUNION!

In an instant, Patrick realised what had happened.
The reverse of being a strict teacher was really
a badly behaved pupil!

"It **IS** you," gasped Patrick. "I recognise
the gingery hair and the long nose."

"Long noses run in our family," explained Ammonia
with a sniff. "Let's go and play some tricks
on all the teachers here. I've got some absolutely
stupendous ideas for causing chaos."

Once Patrick had explained to his class
that Ammonia was really Miss Bunion who had been
turned into a pupil by accident, everyone wanted
to come along and see what she got up to.
"After all," said one boy, "if her skill
at practical jokes is anything like it was
at punishments, the teachers ought
to be in for quite a shock."

First of all Ammonia went to the teachers' car park.
She smeared extra-strong glue on the seat
of Mr Hogget's car and let the air out of his tyres.

Next she went to the staff room.
She put worms in Miss Frustrum's lunch box,
poured ink into Mr Cadenza's hat and hid a frog
in Mrs Majolica's coat pocket.
Finally, she sneaked into the gym, while Miss Biceps
and her class were out jogging. Then she pinched
her huge navy blue knickers and hoisted them
to the top of the flagpole.

"I declare this day to be a school holiday,"
shouted Ammonia. "Let's all skedaddle off home
before we get caught!"

Everyone cheered and ran out of the school gates.
Mr Hogget, the headmaster, tried to chase
after them in his car, but his tyres were flat
and his bottom got stuck on the seat.

Once outside the gates, all of Patrick's class
split up and ran off in different directions,
so they couldn't be caught.
Only Ammonia ran in the same direction as Patrick.

"You've certainly changed," grinned Patrick.
"You've turned into a perfect horror."

"That isn't the only way I've changed,
Patrick darling," replied Ammonia. "I used to
dislike you, but now I want to be your girlfriend."

The grin fell off Patrick's face and was instantly
replaced by an expression of utter dismay.

I hope you're pleased about that, Patrick sweetie,"
she continued, "Because if you're not, the pranks
I'll start playing on you will be a hundred times
worse than anything I could possibly
have done to you as a teacher!"

Patrick could hardly believe it.
It was amazing how whenever things got reversed,
they always seemed to end up even worse
than they had been before.

"Let's see what mischief we can get up to in town,"
suggested Ammonia with a giggle.
"Yesterday, I pinched a baby doll out of a pram
and put it in the hen house at Bramble Farm.
You should have seen the farmer's face
when he came to collect the eggs."

"That doll belongs to my sister!" exclaimed
Patrick. "You'd better give it back to me."
"Why should I?" retorted Ammonia, shoving him.

"How do you think you got changed into a pupil?"
asked Patrick. "Well, I'll tell you," he continued.
"I did it because you were so mean to me yesterday.
And if you don't get my sister's doll back,
I'll turn you into a caterpillar and keep you
in a jam jar!" (He couldn't, of course, but
Ammonia didn't know that. She looked scared stiff
and started being nice again.)

"I'll get it at once, Patrick darling," she said
in a sweet, syrupy voice.
"I'll give it to your dear little sister myself,
when I come round to your house for dinner."

Then before Patrick could say, "Don't you dare,"
she shot round a corner and ran off.

It was still a couple of hours before dinner time,
so Patrick decided to visit the market and look
for Dr Tapioca. More than ever he was beginning
to wish that the effect of the peppermints
could be cancelled.

Things were getting decidedly out of hand.
But, as Lizzy had already discovered,
Dr Tapioca was nowhere to be found. In fact,
no-one had even heard of him.

Finally, Patrick had to give up and go home.
The huge midnight-blue limousine was parked
on the drive and the front door was open.
As he walked in, he heard the most ear-splitting
scream from upstairs. He ran up
and found his mother and sister
standing by the cot reading a note.

"Your father
has kidnapped
Lizzy," wailed
Mrs Marrow.
"I'll never
see her
again unless
I give him
his job back."

"What are you going to do?"
gasped Patrick.

"I don't know," groaned his mother.
She went downstairs still wondering.
She removed her hat, went to hang it in the hall
cupboard, and there, wrapped up in the living room
curtains, she discovered her husband.

"YOU ROTTER!" she yelled, whacking him over
the head with her executive briefcase.
"It's no good trying to hide." Then she realised
he was bound and gagged, so untied him.

"That's three bumps now," he groaned,
tenderly rubbing the top of his head.

"You'd better shut up and explain what's happened,"
replied Mrs Marrow, "Or I'll give you
a fourth lump, for good measure!"

"It's that dotty old Great Aunt of yours,"
he roared. "She's really a master criminal
in disguise. First she kidnapped Lizzy,
then she bashed me on the bean
to stop me from fetching the police."

"I didn't," wailed Lizzy. "It's all Patrick's fault.
He's the one who turned me into an old lady.
Don't you recognize your own daughter? I'm Lizzy!"

At that very moment Ammonia Bunion strolled in
through the front door carrying the doll, which
poor Mrs Marrow mistook for her baby daughter.

"LIZZY!" she cried, snatching the doll. "Arghhhhhh!
What have you done to her, you wicked girl?
She's as tough as a hard boiled egg."

Everyone was shouting at everyone else.
Then just to add to the confusion Bouncer started
barking, and bit Ammonia because she was the only
person he didn't recognize.

Patrick sat on the floor with his head in his hands.

"I wish I'd never been given the rotten peppermints," he groaned. "If only I was incredibly brilliant, I could think of a way to solve everything. But I'm not. I'm just an utter dunce!" Suddenly, it occurred to him - he had thought almost those exact words yesterday, just before Miss Bunion caught him unwrapping the peppermint he had intended to eat himself.

"THAT'S IT!" he shouted. "Then I'll know exactly what to do." He reached into his pocket and pulled out the bag containing the peppermints.
He chose the peppermint with the number six printed on its shiny purple paper, unwrapped it and stuffed it into his mouth.

He chewed it a couple of times and gulped.
As it glided down his throat he felt a deliciously hot and bubbly sensation inside, as if he were a human volcano about to explode.

"Look out," he yelled. "I'm going to go flying!"

Everyone stopped arguing for a moment and turned round to see what Patrick was shouting about. They were only just in time. In an enormous explosion of bright purple smoke, he burst out of the front door and zoomed off into the sky.

CHAPTER TWELVE

PATRICK AND THE PROFESSOR

Patrick shot into the air like a kite
on a windy day, thoroughly enjoying
every single moment of his flight. He found
that by moving his arms or head slightly,
he could steer himself in any direction he wanted.

He did several loops and spirals
and then launched into the clouds like a rocket.
Up and up he soared until his family appeared
to be no bigger than ants, when he looked back down
at them on the ground. All the time,
he was growing steadily older, without even
realising it. His arms and legs grew longer,
and his brain got considerably bigger.

Gradually, he felt himself running out of energy
and the purple smoke seemed to be fading, so he did
a backwards somersault and swooped to the ground.
He landed fairly well for a beginner,
only demolishing the garden fence and a couple
of flower beds.

"MY GIDDY AUNT!" exclaimed Mrs Marrow.
"Is that really you, Patrick?
You look more like a nutty old professor!"

"It's me all right," replied Patrick, staring
at his reflection in the window. He looked
at least sixty years older, tall and lanky,
with a huge domed forehead, long, straggly white
hair and a shaggy moustache. "Now that you've seen
how **I've** changed, perhaps you'll believe that Great
Aunt Elizabeth really **is** your baby daughter!"

Mr and Mrs Marrow said nothing.
They just stared at Patrick
with their mouths hanging open.

"You see," he went on to explain.
"I've just eaten a Reversing Peppermint.
They can reverse absolutely anybody

into the complete opposite of whatever they are.
You've all eaten one, and that's why you've changed
such a lot. The problem is," he said with a sigh,
"the effects are meant to be permanent,
and won't ever wear off."

"So why have you taken one,
you idiotic little blister?" asked Mrs Marrow.
"What good is that going to do **us**?"

"I felt sure there must be some way
to undo all the damage I'd done," said Patrick.
"But I was too stupid to think how."

"You can say that again," interrupted Ammonia.
"You always were a fat-head!"

Patrick glared at Ammonia over the top of his
shaggy white moustache. "That's why I reversed
myself into a really brainy professor,"
he continued. "Now I know exactly what to do."
"Hooray!" cheered Great Aunt Elizabeth,
longing to be her old self again.

"The solution is remarkably easy, when
you're as brainy as this," replied the Professor.
"The only way to turn yourself into the person
you were before, is by taking another peppermint.
Then you would simply reverse right back again.
For example," he continued, unwrapping
the peppermint with the number seven printed
on its shiny pink paper. "The reverse of being
Patrick the Professor, is being Patrick the school
boy. Watch closely and I'll demonstrate."

He popped the seventh peppermint into his mouth,
chewed a few times and swallowed.
In next to no time he was flying through
the air with blazing bright pink smoke streaming
out behind. As he flew around the house,
everyone watched him transform into the Patrick
they recognised. He landed much better
the second time, taxied to a halt, and was greeted
by the loud cheers of his family.

"It's nice to have you back to your old self
again," said Mr Marrow, giving his son a hug.

"I expect he's still as thick
as a plank though," remarked Mrs Marrow.

"Bound to be," agreed Ammonia.

"Who cares anyway?" laughed Lizzy. "Hand round
the peppermints. Let's all get back to normal."

For some mysterious reason Patrick hesitated,
clutching the peppermint bag tightly in his fist,
but Lizzy could stand it no longer.
She grabbed the bag and pulled hard.
Suddenly it ripped completely in two,
and the peppermint with the number eight printed
on its shiny turquoise paper fell on to the ground.

For a moment, time seemed to stand still
as everyone stared in silent horror
at the single peppermint.

At last Mr Marrow cleared his throat,
and spoke in a nervous whisper.
"Is that the last one, son?" he asked.

Patrick nodded.

"You half-baked turnip," grumbled Mrs
Marrow. "That brilliant professor you turned into
wasn't so brainy after all."

"Now only one of us can reverse
back to our old selves again," groaned Ammonia.

"The question is," sighed Lizzy. "Who will it be?"

CHAPTER THIRTEEN

THE LAST PEPPERMINT

Everyone started talking at once.

"I'm not sure I want to change back to exactly
how I was," groaned Mrs Marrow. "I don't want
to be stuck in the house all day long.
I'm good at my new job, and besides, I enjoy being
able to get dressed up and look nice for a change.
Give the peppermint to Ammonia - she's nothing
but a pest, and Patrick needs a good teacher,
or he'll never get any brains."

"I was **never** a good teacher," admitted Ammonia
Bunion. "I was just a Lump of Grump!
Everyone was frightened of me. Children can learn
much more if their lessons are fun.
I realise that now, so I don't want to be exactly
how I was. Give the peppermint to Mr Marrow.
He's so soppy now he's always wearing an apron."

"But I don't think **I** want to change back either,"
said Mr Marrow. "Why should I spend my whole life
cooped up in an office block?
For years I've worked hard to provide a nice house
for my family, but when I get home from the office,
I'm too tired to enjoy it. Doing the housework
makes a pleasant change, and anyway, it gives me
a chance to have fun with the children
while they're growing up. Give the peppermint
to Lizzy - I can't wait to have an adorable
little baby to look after."

"It's true I'm tired of being a grown-up,"
sighed Lizzy. "But I don't want to be a baby again
if there's no one but Dad to care for me.
He never used to hold me properly, and I was scared
he would drop me. And whenever I cried,
he never understood why. He'd just stick my thumb
in my mouth and walk off."

"If Mum can't change back as well, I'd rather stay
as I am. Give the peppermint to Bouncer.
He hasn't got any bounce at all these days.
He behaves more like a robot than a dog.
It used to be so funny when he got into mischief."

Suddenly Bouncer started barking like mad.
He was so clever now, that he understood every
single word that had been spoken, and if only
the humans could have understood **his** language,
they would have found out that **he** didn't want to be
exactly as he used to be either.
People were always shouting at him when he got
into trouble, or smacking him with a rolled-up
newspaper. But unfortunately, as no one could
understand him, Mr Marrow shouted at him to
"Shut up!" and Mrs Marrow sloshed him
with her copy of the Financial Times!

"Don't worry," smiled Patrick. "None of you needs
to reverse back to exactly the way you were.
I don't want you to be like that again anyway.
You were absolutely awful. Why do you think
I gave you the peppermints in the first place?"

"Then **who** is going to eat the last one?" asked Ammonia.

"All of you," replied Patrick. "While I was still incredibly brainy, I worked out a mind-blowing mathematical equation that gave me the answer."

"Well, don't just stand there waffling, you gormless gumboil," scolded his mother. "Tell us!"

"If you only eat **part** of a peppermint, then only **part** of you will be reversed," explained Patrick. "Because you are getting such a small dose of Reversing Peppermint, it will only be strong enough to change the things you really want to change about yourselves. Anything you don't want to change will stay just as it is!"

"I think I understand," said Mr Marrow. "If your theory is correct, the bad things about us will be reversed into good things, while the good things will remain exactly as they are."

"I've just remembered a poem I used to recite at school," gasped Ammonia. "Part of it said that 'we need to have the courage to change the things we can, the serenity to accept the things we can't change and the wisdom to know the difference,' or something like that."

"Yes," agreed Mr Marrow. "It sounds quite logical. But will it really work?"

"There's only one way to find out!"
shouted Patrick, as he ran into the house.

He hurried back with a sharp pair of scissors,
and cut the last remaining peppermint
into five equal pieces. One each for Mr Marrow,
Mrs Marrow, Lizzy, Ammonia and Bouncer.

They each gobbled their bit of peppermint
and waited anxiously for that deliciously hot
and bubbly feeling deep inside them,
as if they were human volcanoes about to erupt.

But nothing happened.

"Don't worry," said Patrick.
"I expect smaller doses take longer to work.

He was right. While they were having tea,
they noticed that Great Aunt Elizabeth was starting
to look a little younger and Ammonia Bunion
was starting to look a little older.

At the end of the meal, Mr Marrow washed the dishes
while his wife dried them.
Then they all sat together in the lounge, laughing
about the peculiar adventures they had been having.

When it got late, Mr and Mrs Marrow invited Ammonia
to stay the night in the spare bedroom.

Exhausted, they all went to sleep,
wondering just how much they would have changed
by the following morning.

When Mrs Marrow woke up, she was
the same gentle and motherly person she used to be.
She wanted to spend time at home with Lizzy
instead of working all day in an office,
but she didn't want to give up her new job
completely.

When Mr Marrow woke up he felt much more
business-like again. Instead of being the mean
and bombastic person he used to be, he was still

kind and considerate. He wished he could have
his job back at the office, but he still wanted
to share the responsibility of homemaking
and looking after the children.

For the first time in many years, the two of them
talked about their future plans together.
Mrs Marrow decided to invite her husband
to join her as co-director of the company,
and they changed the name to M.O.F. Co.,
which stood for Marrow's Ozone Friendly Company.
They made sure that all their factories stopped
polluting the environment, and made only things
that could be recycled.

The two of them soon found that they enjoyed
working together, both in the office **and** at home.

Mr Marrow was proud to have a wife who was such
a clever business woman **and** a good mother,
so he suggested that there should be a day nursery
in each factory. Women and men workers could work,
even if they also had to look after children.

Mrs Marrow was proud to have a husband
who was always willing to do his share at home.
She was especially proud of their beautiful garden.
Now that Mr Marrow had more time at home,
he discovered he had a gift for making things grow.
So they always had fresh flowers
on the kitchen table and were never short
of delicious organic vegetables.

Every Saturday they would both take the whole day
off, to do something special with their children.
Sometimes they would go swimming at the beach,
or camping in the mountains.
They would fly kites in the park, ride horses,
take Bouncer for a really good, long walk,
or do anything at all, as long as they were all together.

Lizzy reversed into a baby again.
This time she was the quietest and best behaved
little girl you could ever hope to meet.

Ammonia Bunion turned back into a teacher,
only now she was a nice, kind teacher, who really
liked children. She was lots of fun and always
thought of exciting ways to teach things to her
pupils. In fact, during the very next school
holidays, she took the entire class on a trip to
Egypt to help them learn all about the Pyramids.

Bouncer reversed into the scruffy old dog he had
been before. And, although he never set the table,
or fetched Mr Marrow's slippers again,
he always walked obediently to heel,
and stopped tiddling on people's feet!

Only Patrick was exactly the same
as he had been before.

Well, not quite the same.

Now that he had wonderful parents,
an adorable baby sister, a kind teacher
and an obedient dog, he wasn't miserable
or sorry for himself any longer.
In fact, he enjoyed just about everything,

except for perhaps, one small thing...

... He was never very keen on peppermints!

THE END